WILDA'S GENERAL STORE ADVENTURE

by Michael Scotto

illustrated by The Ink Circle

WELCOME TO MIDLANDIA

OUR STORY BEGINS

HERE

Midlandia University

Community Center

Playland Park

Animal Land

To Town

Bike Factory

Harvest Farms

Wilda was the zookeeper of Animal Land in Midlandia. Her job was to make sure that the tigers, the monkeys, the giraffes, and all of the other animals that lived there were well fed and had plenty of space to roam.

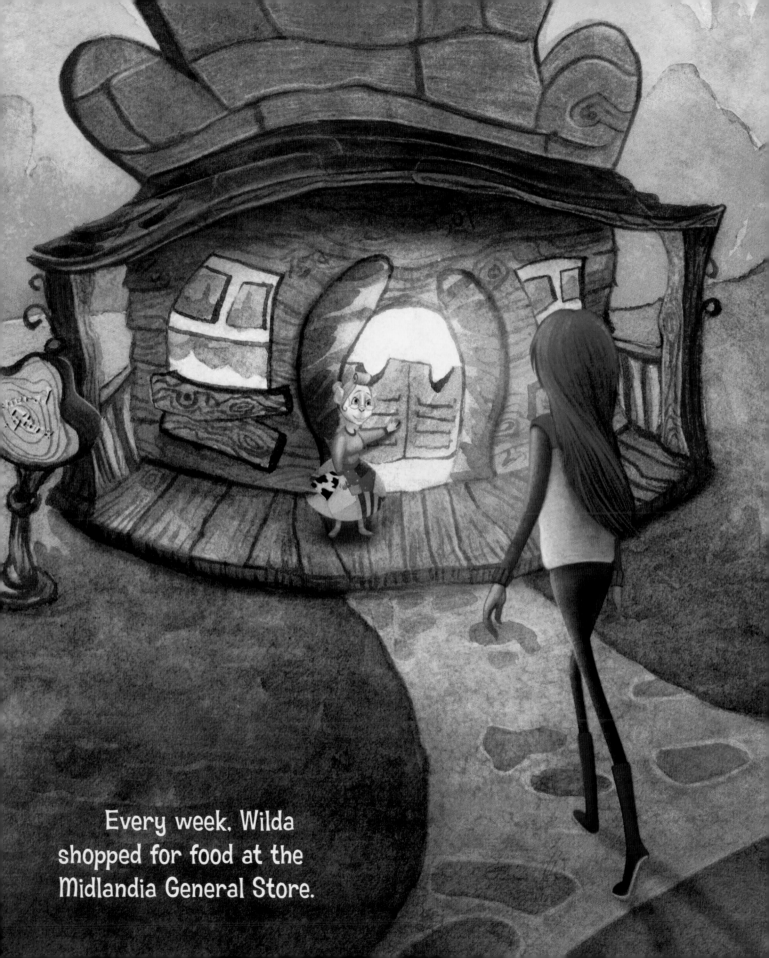

Every week, Wilda
shopped for food at the
Midlandia General Store.

Wilda always tried to get the animals' favorite foods.

"Bananas for the monkeys,

peanuts for the elephants,

carrots for the zebras,

and apples for the giraffes...."

If she couldn't find something she wanted, she would ask Scannit politely for help. "Excuse me...can you tell me where I can find the Brussels sprouts? Larry the lion loves Brussels sprouts!"

"Go to aisle seven," Scannit said. "You'll find them right by the apples." Scannit owned the general store. He knew just as much about his store as Wilda did about her zoo.

It took Wilda most of the afternoon to find the favorite food of each animal. "I'd better get back soon," Wilda thought. "The chinchillas are afraid of the dark."

Suddenly, from behind the corn flakes, Wilda heard a whisper. **"Psst!"**

It was an Ink!

"Who are you?"
Wilda asked.
"A friend," he said slyly.

Wilda had never met him before. "What kind of friend?" she wondered. The Ink gave a grin and said, "The kind of friend who helps you with things."

"Well, I could use some help today," Wilda sighed. "If the kangaroos don't have their dinner on time, they get very cranky."

The Ink scurried closer. "I know what you can do," he whispered. "Just walk out the door."

"You think I should leave without paying?" Wilda exclaimed. **"Shhh, not so loud,"** the Ink said. "If you're in a hurry, Scannit won't mind. Just skip past the line and run home."

"Well," Wilda replied, "it would help me save some time...." **"Then hurry up!"** said the Ink, and he tossed a box of powdered sugar on the floor, where it burst open in a cloud of dust.

"Oh!" cried Wilda. "I'm not sure you should be doing that."
"I can do whatever I want!"
He flopped on his back and made a powdered sugar angel.
"The supermarket sure is fun!" he said.

But then a voice came from the end of the aisle. "Whoa! Hold on there, little partner!"

Wilda hurried to Scannit, her face red with embarrassment.
"Scannit, I'm glad you're here! I wasn't sure what to do." She
pointed to the Ink. "He was saying I should leave without paying."

Scannit leaned over the Ink as the rascal dusted himself off.

"Is that true?" Scannit asked.

The Ink looked from side to side.
"Um...I have to go now."

The Ink kicked up a cloud of sugar and dashed away.

"Those critters are always causing trouble," Scannit said as he mopped up the sugar. "I'm so confused," Wilda said. "Can you tell me what I should do?"

"At the supermarket," Scannit explained, "you have to get in line and wait your turn. If someone gets in line before you, it's only fair that he or she goes first, even if you're in a hurry."

Wilda took her place in line and waited for her turn.

At the checkout counter, Scannit picked up each item from Wilda's cart. "Thanks for waiting," Scannit said. He used his scanner to find out how much each item cost. "You have to pay for each item you pick out," he said. "So I check each one to make sure I don't charge you too much or too little."

After paying her bill, Wilda said, "I'd better get home before the monkeys make a mess. Since you were such a big help, next time you come to Animal Land I'll give you a tour!" "No trouble at all ma'am," Scannit said as he waved goodbye.

Back at Animal Land, Wilda served dinner. The monkeys clapped, the kangaroos hopped, the chinchillas chirped...and that night the whole zoo went to sleep with full, happy bellies.

DISCUSSION QUESTIONS

What is your favorite food to buy at the grocery store?

How do you feel when someone cuts in line?

Do you think it is wrong to take something
and not pay for it? Why?